This book belongs to

_____

WALT DISNEY

VOLUME 12

SCROOGE
AND THE MAGIC FISH

WALT DISNEY FUN-TO-READ LIBRARY

Donald Duck was always busy.
He worked in Uncle Scrooge's money bin.
He cleaned the coins. He ironed the dollar
bills. He raked the money so it would be in
neat piles.

One day Donald went to Uncle Scrooge
to ask for more pay. "I work hard," said
Donald. "I should have more money."

"More money?" said Scrooge. "I cannot give you more money. I am only a poor old duck."

"You are <u>not</u> a poor old duck!" cried Donald. "You have lots of money. Your money bin is full of money."

"My money bin is not full," said Scrooge.
"It is half-empty. I <u>am</u> only a poor old duck!"
    With that, Uncle Scrooge put on his hat
and went out.

"Donald does not understand me,"
said Scrooge to himself. "I will go to
the Millionaires' Club. The people there
understand me."

When he got to the Millionaires' Club,
Uncle Scrooge saw a sign. "Fishing Contest
for Club Members," it said. "Catch the biggest
fish. Win your weight in gold!"

"What a great contest!" said Scrooge. "I
will enter it this minute!"

And he did.

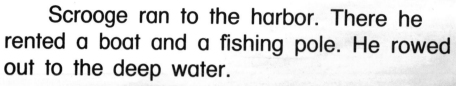

Scrooge ran to the harbor. There he rented a boat and a fishing pole. He rowed out to the deep water.

In no time at all, Scrooge felt a nibble on the line. He pulled in a very big fish. "What a whopper!" he cried. "I will win the contest for sure!"

Suddenly the fish began to talk. "Please," said he, "throw me back into the sea."

"What?" cried Uncle Scrooge. "Throw you back? Nonsense! You are worth money. No one throws away money."

"If you throw me back, I will give you your dearest wish," said the fish.

"Hmmmm!" thought Scrooge. "A talking fish must be a magic fish. Perhaps this fish really can give me my dearest wish."

So Uncle Scrooge wished to have his money bin filled to the very top.

"You have your wish," said the fish. "Go home and look at your money bin."
Uncle Scrooge threw the fish back into the sea. Then he rowed to the shore.

Uncle Scrooge ran to his money bin. Lo
and behold, the money bin was full. It was so
full that gold pieces and hundred dollar bills
were piled up to the ceiling.

"I don't understand it, Uncle Scrooge,"
said Donald. "I was just cleaning a few coins.
Suddenly all this money appeared."

Uncle Scrooge jumped with joy. "Oh, what a lucky duck I am!" he cried.

But soon he began to think. "Did I make
a mistake?" he wondered. "A fish who can fill
a money bin can surely do more. I was too
quick to let that fish off the hook."

Back to the harbor ran Uncle Scrooge. He rowed out to the deep water. He called to the fish.

"Oh, fish," he called. "It is Scrooge
McDuck. I want to have a word with you."

"What now?" asked the fish. "Isn't your money bin full?"

"It is," said Uncle Scrooge. "But I would like another small favor. May I have a palace? It does not seem right that I have so much money and still live in the same old place."

"Very well," said the fish. "You now have a palace. Go home, and try to be happy."

The fish swam off. Scrooge went home.
His house was gone. In its place was a
beautiful palace. It had golden doors and
marble floors.

"I don't know what happened, Uncle Scrooge," said Donald. "I was just dusting the table, the way I always do. Suddenly your house was gone."

"Don't worry, Donald," said Uncle Scrooge. "You have an uncle who is smart as well as lucky."

Scrooge was happy with his palace for about half an hour. Then he had a new idea.

"Since I have a palace," said he, "I should be a king. I should sit on a throne. I should wear a gold crown."

"Uncle Scrooge, you are being silly!" said Donald.

Scrooge did not listen. He ran back to
the harbor. He rowed out to the deep water.
He called to the fish.

"What now?" asked the fish. "Is there something wrong with your palace?"

"It is a grand palace," said Scrooge. "It is fit for a king. King Scrooge the First, that is."

"What nonsense!" said the fish.

"Is that the thanks I get?" said Scrooge. "After all, I did let you go!"

"Very well," said the fish. "I will give you this wish, too. Go home, and try to be a good king."

Scrooge thanked the fish, and he hurried home.

When Scrooge returned to his palace,
there were many servants waiting for him.
They bowed when he came in.
"Your wish is our command, oh king,"
the head servant told him.

At the end of the hall was the throne.
Scrooge proudly sat on it.
On the throne was a crown of gold.
Scrooge put it on his head.

"Donald," said Scrooge, "run down to the Millionaires' Club. Tell the members that His Majesty, Scrooge McDuck, commands them to come to the palace. They will be green with envy when they see it."

"I don't think so," said Donald. "I think they will laugh their heads off."

"Don't you dare talk that way to your king!" said Scrooge.

Then Scrooge thought that perhaps
a king was not mighty enough.

"I should be an emperor," he said,
"emperor of all the world. Then no one
would dare to laugh at me."

Back to the sea went Uncle Scrooge. He called out to the magic fish.

Dark clouds suddenly hid the sun. The sea turned gray. A cold wind blew.

At last the fish lifted his head from the water. "Well?" he asked.

"Being a king is not grand enough for me," said Scrooge. "I must be an emperor. Emperors are really grand!"

"Is there no end to your greed?" asked the fish. "Money, a palace—even being king has not made you happy. I know now there is no magic strong enough to make a greedy person happy. Go home. Be content with what you had before you ever met me."

And the fish swam away.

Uncle Scrooge went home. His palace
was gone. So were his throne and his crown.
All that was left was a sad Donald Duck.

"I don't know what happened, Uncle
Scrooge," said Donald. "All of a sudden the
palace was gone. And now the money bin is
half-empty again."

Uncle Scrooge began to cry. He cried for his gold crown and his lost kingdom. He cried for the heaps of money that had disappeared.

"I am only a poor old duck once again!" he sobbed.

After a while, Uncle Scrooge remembered what the fish had said. "There is no magic strong enough to make a greedy person happy. Be content with what you have."

He dried his eyes. "Perhaps my money bin is not half-empty, but half-full. Maybe I am not so poor after all."

Donald could hardly believe his ears.
"That was a wise fish," said Scrooge.
"Now you just follow me, Donald. We are
going out to dinner."

They did go out to dinner. They laughed
and had a lot of good things to eat. But when
they were finished, Uncle Scrooge handed
Donald the bill.

He was still the same old Scrooge
McDuck—even though a magic fish had
taught him a lesson!